CESAR CHAVEZ

A Real-Life Reader Biography

Susan Zannos

Mitchell Lane Publishers, Inc.
P.O. Box 619
Bear, Delaware 19701

Mitchell Lane
PUBLISHERS

Third Printing

Real-Life Reader Biographies

Paula Abdul	Mary Joe Fernandez	Ricky Martin	Arnold Schwarzenegger
Christina Aguilera	Andres Galarraga	Mark McGwire	Selena
Marc Anthony	Sarah Michelle Gellar	Alyssa Milano	Maurice Sendak
Drew Barrymore	Jeff Gordon	Mandy Moore	Dr. Seuss
Brandy	Mia Hamm	Chuck Norris	Shakira
Garth Brooks	Melissa Joan Hart	Tommy Nuñez	Alicia Silverstone
Kobe Bryant	Faith Hill	Rosie O'Donnell	Jessica Simpson
Sandra Bullock	Jennifer Love Hewitt	Rafael Palmeiro	Sinbad
Mariah Carey	Hollywood Hogan	Gary Paulsen	Sammy Sosa
Cesar Chavez	Katie Holmes	Freddie Prinze, Jr.	Britney Spears
Christopher Paul Curtis	Enrique Iglesias	Julia Roberts	Sheryl Swoopes
Roald Dahl	Derek Jeter	Robert Rodriguez	Shania Twain
Oscar De La Hoya	Steve Jobs	J.K. Rowling	Liv Tyler
Trent Dimas	Michelle Kwan	Keri Russell	Robin Williams
Celine Dion	Bruce Lee	Winona Ryder	Vanessa Williams
Sheila E.	Jennifer Lopez	Cristina Saralegui	Tiger Woods
Gloria Estefan	Cheech Marin		

Library of Congress Cataloging-in-Publication Data
Zannos, Susan.
    Cesar Chavez / Susan Zannos.
      p. cm.—(A real-life reader biography)
    Includes index.
    Summary: A biography of the Mexican American who spent most of his life working to organize migrant farm workers in California and was instrumental in the founding of the United Farm Workers union.
    ISBN 1-883845-71-8
    1. Chavez, Cesar, 1927–1993 —Juvenile literature. 2. Labor leaders—United States—Biography—Juvenile literature. 3. Strikes and lockouts—Agricultural laborers—California—Juvenile literature. 4. National Farm Workers Association—Juvenile literature. 5. United Farm Workers Organization Committee—Juvenile literature. [1. Chavez, Cesar, 1927–1993. 2. Labor leaders. 3. Mexican Americans—Biography. 4. Migrant labor. 5. United Farm Workers.] I. Title. II. Series.
HD6509.C48Z36 1998
331.88′13′092—dc21
[B]
                                                        98-30665
                                                         CIP
                                                         AC

ABOUT THE AUTHOR: Susan Zannos has taught at all levels, from preschool to college, in Mexico, Greece, Italy, Russia, and Lithuania, as well as in the United States. She has published a mystery **Trust the Liar** (Walker and Co.) and **Human Types: Essence and the Enneagram** was published by Samuel Weiser in 1997. She has written several books for children, including **Paula Abdul** (Mitchell Lane).

PHOTO CREDITS: cover: Corbis-Bettmann; p. 4 Bill Warren/Globe Photos; p. 19 Cesar E. Chavez Foundation; p. 20 Globe Photos; pp. 23, 24, 26, 28, 29 UPI/Corbiss-Bettmann; pp. 30, 31 Cesar E. Chavez Foundation

ACKNOWLEDGMENTS: The following story has been approved by the Cesar E. Chavez Foundation in Keene, CA.

Table of Contents

Chapter 1
The Farm

When Cesar Chavez was a boy, he lived on a farm near Yuma, Arizona. Cesar's family was not rich, but they always had enough to eat. They raised chickens and pigs and cows. They grew vegetables and fruit.

Cesar's grandfather came to the United States from Mexico over 100 years ago. Shortly after he arrived, he had enough money to send for his wife and 14 children. Cesar's father, Librado, was only

When Cesar Chavez was a boy, he lived on a farm near Yuma, Arizona.

two years old when his family came to the United States in 1888.

At that time it was possible to get free land by working on it. The Chavez family farmed more than 100 acres. By 1912, when Arizona became the 48th state, many of Cesar's aunts, uncles, and cousins lived in their own homes close to the family farm.

Librado Chavez worked on the farm until he married Cesar's mother, Juana, in 1924. Cesar's parents bought a grocery store near the farm. Cesar was born in the apartment above the store on March 31, 1927.

Cesar's mother was a very religious woman. She taught her children to help the poor. She would send Cesar and his brother Richard out to bring hungry men home for a meal. Cesar's mother

The Chavez family farmed more than 100 acres. Many of their relatives lived nearby.

also taught her children that fighting was wrong. "Turn the other cheek," she said. "It takes two to fight. One cannot do it alone."

It wasn't easy for Cesar not to fight. Some things made him angry. He didn't like school. It was hard to learn English. The teachers punished the children for speaking Spanish. They told them, "If you want to speak Spanish, go back to Mexico."

Cesar's father was having problems, too. The whole country was suffering from the Great Depression, and people could not find work. Even though Cesar's father owned his own business, his customers were very poor. Librado Chavez would let them have food when they promised to pay later. When his customers could not pay,

Cesar's mother taught all her children that fighting was wrong.

Cesar's father could not pay his bills. Soon he had to sell the store.

Cesar's family tried to keep the farm going, but there was no rain for the crops. Nothing would grow. The family was not able to pay the taxes they owed on the land.

In 1939, the Chavez farm was sold to pay the taxes.

Librado Chavez tried to borrow money to pay the taxes. But the man who owned the bank wanted the Chavez farm for himself. He wouldn't loan Cesar's father any money. In 1939 the farm was sold to pay the taxes. A tractor came and destroyed the fences and canals that all of the Chavez family had worked to build. Cesar and his brothers and sisters watched helplessly.

Chapter 2
The Fields

Cesar was 12 years old when his mother and father packed their five children and some clothes and blankets into the back seat of their old car. Like more than 300,000 others who had also lost their jobs and their land, they had no home and no money. They moved from place to place in California, hoping to find jobs working in the fields.

The growers, men who owned the land, needed workers to plant their lettuce and onions, to hoe their fields of vegetables, and to pick

Cesar was 12 years old when his mother and father lost the farm.

A contractor found Cesar's family a job. But when the family finished picking all the grapes, the contractor disap— peared with their money.

their grapes and strawberries. The growers wanted to make a lot of money. They didn't want to pay the workers very much. Because there were so many migrant workers, the growers could always find people willing to work for very little money.

Men called labor contractors found workers for the growers. Sometimes these men cheated the workers. A contractor found Cesar's family a job. The Chavezes picked grapes day after day in the hot sun without water to drink. Each week the contractor gave them only a little money to buy food. He said they would be paid a lot when the job was done. But when the grapes were all picked, the contractor disappeared. He took the money the Chavez family had earned, and they had nothing.

Cesar and his family couldn't find decent places to live. Sometimes they had to live in their car. The first winter they didn't have enough money to rent a room, so they lived in a tent. Cesar and Richard and their cousin Manuel had to sleep outside on the ground because there wasn't enough room for everyone in the tent.

Cesar's family and the other migrant workers followed the crops around California. In summer they picked cucumbers, lettuce, tomatoes, prunes, peaches, and grapes. In the fall they picked cotton.

Because they moved so often, Cesar had to go to different schools. By the time he was in eighth grade, he had gone to 37 schools. Many times the teachers and other students were cruel to the Mexican-

Cesar's family and other migrant workers followed the crops around California.

American children. At one school in Fresno, the principal told Cesar and Richard that none of the teachers wanted them in their classes.

Cesar and sister Vicky when they were young

Chapter 3
Organizing

Cesar Chavez did not go to school past the eighth grade. When he was 17, in 1944, he joined the navy. He had problems there because he often spoke Spanish and had brown skin. He was exposed to much racism while in the navy, though the keen discipline that the navy taught him served him well in the future.

When Cesar was 17, he joined the navy.

Cesar experienced many forms of racism elsewhere. He saw signs in restaurants that said, "No dogs or Mexicans allowed." In theaters there were only certain places where people with dark skin could sit. Once in a movie in Delano, California, Cesar sat in the section reserved for whites. The police came and arrested him.

He knew that the things he experienced were wrong. He wanted to change them. But he remembered what his mother taught him. He could not use violence.

In 1948, Cesar married Helen Fabela, a girl he had met in Delano. He and Helen moved around California, looking for work. They went to San Jose, where his brother Richard was working on an apricot ranch.

In San Jose, Cesar Chavez met two men who changed his life. The first was a Catholic priest, Father McDonnell. Cesar and this priest talked about men like St. Francis and Mahatma Gandhi, who worked for their people using nonviolent methods. The second man was Fred Ross, a man who helped poor people work together to improve their lives. Father McDonnell told Ross about Cesar.

At first Cesar didn't want to talk to this white man. He didn't trust him. But Fred Ross came back again and again, and finally Cesar talked with him. That night Ross wrote, "I think I've found the guy I've been looking for."

Every night, after working all day, Cesar would go out with Fred Ross. They helped people register to vote or get citizenship papers or work permits. Cesar helped people with their problems. The migrant workers trusted him because he was one of them. He knew their

Migrant workers trusted Cesar because he was one of them.

problems, their work, and their language. Cesar learned that poor people can have power when they work together. When the workers registered to vote, they could vote for people who would make laws to help them.

Fred Ross worked for the Community Service Organization, or CSO, and before long Cesar did, too. Even though he was young, he was good at organizing. At first he didn't think people would listen to him. When he went to his first meeting alone, he was so nervous he drove around the block several times before he got up enough courage to walk up to the door.

Cesar went to Oxnard while he was working for the CSO. He found that the growers there were hiring workers who came from Mexico on buses. The workers who lived in

Cesar worked for Fred Ross at the Community Service Organization.

Oxnard could not get jobs because the Mexicans would work for less money.

Cesar helped the workers in Oxnard protest against the use of Mexican workers. They burned their work cards and had a protest march. Newspapers and television programs told about the problem. Finally the government told the growers they had to hire the workers who lived in Oxnard.

Chapter 4
Strike!

By 1958 Cesar Chavez was the general director of the CSO. Cesar knew that the best way to help workers was to get them better pay and better working conditions. Again and again he asked the CSO to let him work with labor problems. Again and again they said no.

In 1962 Cesar quit his job. He knew he had to help the workers form a union. He was worried about how his family would live without his paycheck. He and

By 1958, Cesar was the general director of the CSO.

Helen and their children moved to Delano to be near her family. Helen went back to work in the fields to support the family.

Cesar knew that organizing a union would be hard. Other people had tried and failed. But he also knew how he had helped organize the CSO. He talked to the workers one at a time. Then he met with

The Chavez family, from left to right: standing— Anna, Eloise, Sylvia, Helen, Cesar; sitting— Paul, Elizabeth, and Anthony. Missing from picture: Fernando and Linda

Organization rally in Salinas, California

them in small groups. When there were enough small groups, he held a bigger meeting.

He asked his brother Richard and his cousin Manuel to come and help. They had good jobs by then. They didn't want to be poor again. They said they would help for a while, but they came and stayed.

By 1965 there were 1,200 families in the National Farm Workers Association (NFWA). Cesar thought it would be many more years before they were strong enough to take action as a union.

The Mexican-American migrant workers were not the only ones trying to get better working conditions. Two thousand Filipino grape pickers had voted to strike, which means they would refuse to pick grapes until the growers paid them more. They knew that they couldn't win unless the Mexican-American pickers joined them.

The NFWA held a big meeting. Even though Cesar thought they were not ready, they voted to join the strike. The Delano grape strike began. It lasted for five years.

Cesar knew that the workers had to use nonviolent actions if

If the growers could not sell their grapes, they would have to give up and pay the workers a fair wage.

they were going to win. He sent workers all over the country to ask the people not to buy grapes. The refusal to buy a product is called a boycott. He knew that if the growers could not sell their grapes, they would have to give up and pay the workers a fair wage. Another nonviolent method the strikers used was a 300-mile march from Delano to the state capitol in Sacramento.

Finally, some of the growers gave up and signed a contract to pay the farm workers more money. The Filipinos and the Mexican-Americans joined together to make one bigger and stronger union, the United Farm Workers, or UFW. More and more growers signed contracts with the farm workers.

There were other growers, however, who would not sign

contracts. Some of the strikers talked about using violent methods to make these growers give up. Cesar wouldn't let them. He began a fast, which means he went without eating. He did not eat anything for 25 days. This won support from people all over the country, because they realized how

On March 10, 1968, Senator Robert Kennedy (left) breaks bread with Cesar Chavez at the end of Chavez's fast in support of the strike against grape growers.

On July 29, 1970, Cesar Chavez (left) and John Giumarra Sr., who represented 26 of California's largest table grape growers, exchanged pens to sign a contract with the United Farm Workers Union.

much Cesar was willing to suffer to help the workers.

More people joined the grape boycott. Finally, after five years of the strike, 85 percent of California grapes were being picked by union labor. The boycott and the strike ended.

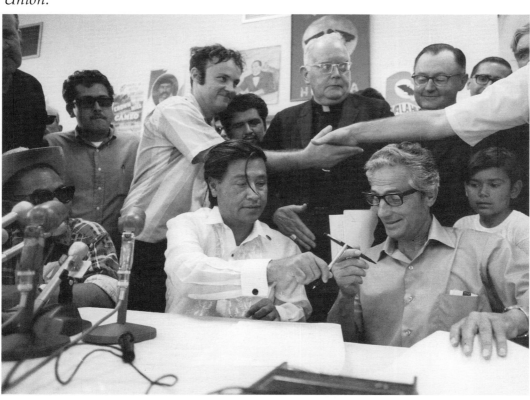

Chapter 5
The Struggle Goes On

When they saw how strong the UFW was, the lettuce and other vegetable growers signed contracts instead with the powerful Teamsters Union. The growers wanted to stop their workers from joining the UFW. With Cesar Chavez leading them, most of the vegetable workers went on strike.

The struggle went on for years. Now Cesar was fighting not only the growers but also the Teamsters Union as well. Later, during other strikes in the grape vineyards,

As the UFW got stronger, many growers signed contracts with the Teamsters instead.

On November 8, 1979, Cesar led a band of pickets at a busy intersection near the Golden Gate Bridge and waved signs at commuters during the busy morning rush hour. He urged a boycott of lettuce because more than a dozen Salinas growers were using illegal workers to break the 10-month UFW strike.

violence broke out. Two striking workers were killed. But Cesar Chavez did not give up. He continued to use nonviolent protest.

In 1975 the State of California passed the Agricultural Labor Relations Act. This was the first law protecting the right of farm workers to organize. It was a big victory for Cesar Chavez. It meant that legally the growers could no longer refuse to accept the United Farm Workers as the union the migrant workers wanted.

Cesar got many new contracts with the growers after workers voted for the UFW in elections. Not only did the workers get more pay, but they also got medical care and other benefits. Even workers at nonunion farms were treated better because the growers were afraid the workers would join the UFW.

In 1975, California passed a law protecting the right of farm—workers to organize.

In 1987, Cesar spoke at a press conference in Washington, DC concerning a United Farm Workers' boycott of "poison" grapes. Cesar asked for a ban of five pesticides (chemicals used to kill bugs) used on grapes that were linked to cancer, birth defects, and other illnesses.

Although many victories had been won, there were still many serious problems. One of the greatest dangers the farm workers faced was the use of pesticides. These poisons, which kill insects, were sprayed on the crops while the workers were in the fields. Many of the workers became seriously ill.

In 1988, when he was 61 years old, Cesar Chavez started another fast to protest the use of pesticides. This time Cesar went 36 days without eating.

On August 21, 1988, Cesar broke his 36-day fast. Here, he holds Jesse Jackson's hand during a mass in Delano.

Cesar continued to work for better conditions for the farm workers until he died. He traveled all over the country to help people understand how to organize and

With his mother, Juana

act nonviolently to change their lives.

Cesar Chavez died in his sleep on April 23, 1993. He was 66 years old. Many people thought the farm workers' union would not continue without Cesar to lead it. They were wrong.

The next year, on March 31, 1994, Cesar's birthday, the UFW again marched from Delano to Sacramento as they had done nearly 30 years before. The marchers demonstrated the strength of the UFW. They showed that Cesar's dream of a national union of farm workers is possible.

An estimated fifty-thousand people followed Cesar's casket in a three-mile march from Memorial Park in Delano, California to the funeral mass at the United Farm Worker's field office west of town.

Chronology

- 1927, born on March 31 near Yuma, Arizona
- 1939, Chavez farm was sold and family became migrant workers
- 1944–1946, served in the U.S. Navy
- 1948, married Helen Fabela of Delano, California, on October 22
- 1952, began working for the Community Service Organization (CSO)
- 1958, named general director of the CSO
- 1962, left CSO to begin National Farm Workers Association
- 1965, Delano grape pickers' strike began
- 1966, marched with farmworkers from Delano to Sacramento
- 1968, began 25-day fast on February 14
- 1970, grape boycott and strike ended
- 1975, Agricultural Labor Relations Act passed in California
- 1984, second grape boycott organized
- 1988, 36-day fast to protest use of pesticides
- 1993, died at the age of 66 on April 23

Index